Cataloging-in-Publication Data (by Cassidy Cataloging)

Otoshi, Kathryn
One [and] Zero / by Kathryn Otoshi -- Dual special ed. (Tete-beche) -- San Rafael, CA : KO Kids Books, c2011.
    p. ; cm.
    ISBN: 978-0-9723946-5-9 (pbk)
    Combined reissuing of the author's One (c2008) and Zero (c2010).
    Summary for One: a number/color book reminding us that it just takes one to make everyone count.
    Summary for Zero: One character's search to find value in herself and in others.

    1. Bullying--Juvenile fiction. 2. Courage--Juvenile fiction.
    3. Colors--Juvenile fiction. 4. Counting--Juvenile fiction.
    5. Values--Juvenile fiction. 6. Social skills--Juvenile fiction.
    7. [Bullies--Fiction. 8. Courage--Fiction. 9. Color--Fiction.
    10. Counting--Fiction. 11. Values--Fiction. 12. Social skills--Fiction.]
    I. Otoshi, Kathryn. One. II. Otoshi, Kathryn. Zero. III. Title.

PZ7.O8775 O542 2011
[Fic]--dc22   1104

KO KIDS BOOKS
16 Baytree Rd.
San Rafael, CA 94903
www.kokidsbooks.com

Printed in China

One

by Kathryn Otoshi

Blue was a quiet color.

He enjoyed looking up at the sky,

floating on the waves,

and on days he felt daring...
splashing in rain puddles.

Every once in a while he wished he could be more sunny like Yellow.

Or bright like **Green**.

More regal like **Purple**.

Or outgoing like **Orange**.

But overall, he liked being **Blue**...

except when he was with **Red**.

Red was a hot head.
He liked to pick on **Blue**.

"Red is a great color," he'd say. "Red is hot. Blue is not."

Then **Blue** would feel bad about being **Blue**.

Sometimes Yellow comforted Blue.

"Blue is a very nice color," she'd say.

But Yellow never said that in front of Red.

She never said, "Stop picking on Blue!"

Green, **Purple** and **Orange**
thought **Blue** was nice too,
but they never told **Red** to stop either.

Every time **Red** said something mean
and no one spoke up, he got...

bigger...

and **bigger...**

and **BIGGER...**

Soon **Red** grew so big that *everyone* was afraid of him.

No one dared stop him.

Red picked on *all* the colors.

Then everyone felt...a little **blue**.

Until **One** came.

He had a different shape with bold strokes and squared corners.

He was funny.

He made the colors laugh.

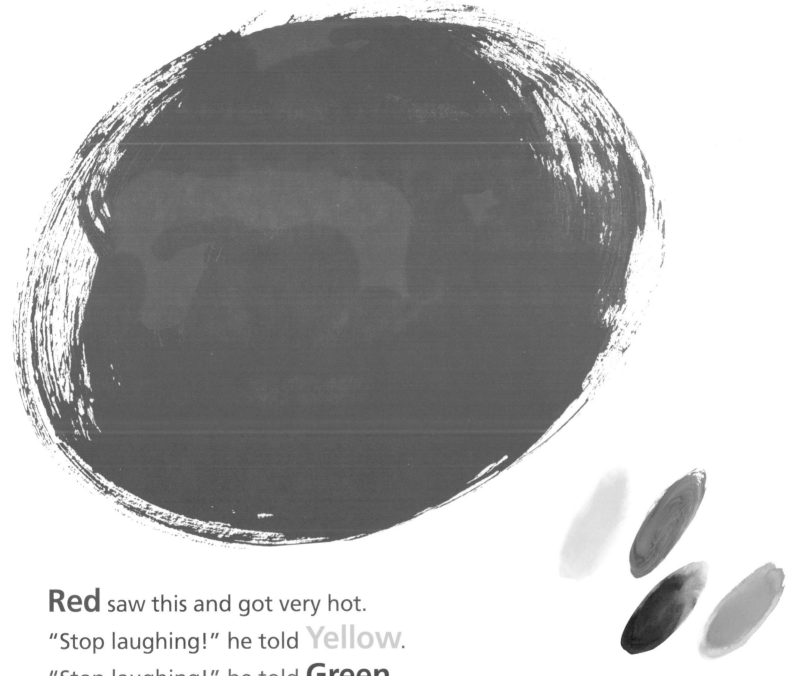

Red saw this and got very hot.

"Stop laughing!" he told Yellow.

"Stop laughing!" he told **Green**.

"Stop laughing!" he told **Purple** and Orange.

And they did.

Red rolled up to **One**.

"Stop laughing!" he told him.

But **One** stood up straight like an arrow and said, *"No."*

Red was mad, but **One** wouldn't budge. So **Red** rolled away.

One turned to the colors and said,
"If someone is mean and picks on me,
I, for One, stand up and say, *No.*"

Then Yellow felt brave and said, "Me TWO!"

Green agreed and said, "Me THREE!"

Then **Purple** became **FOUR**.

And **Orange** became **FIVE**.

Blue saw the colors change.
He wanted to *count*.

Red grew red hot. He felt left out.
He grew **hotter** and **hotter** and **HOTTER**.

Red raced over to **Blue** and said what he always did.
"Red is HOT. Blue is NOT."

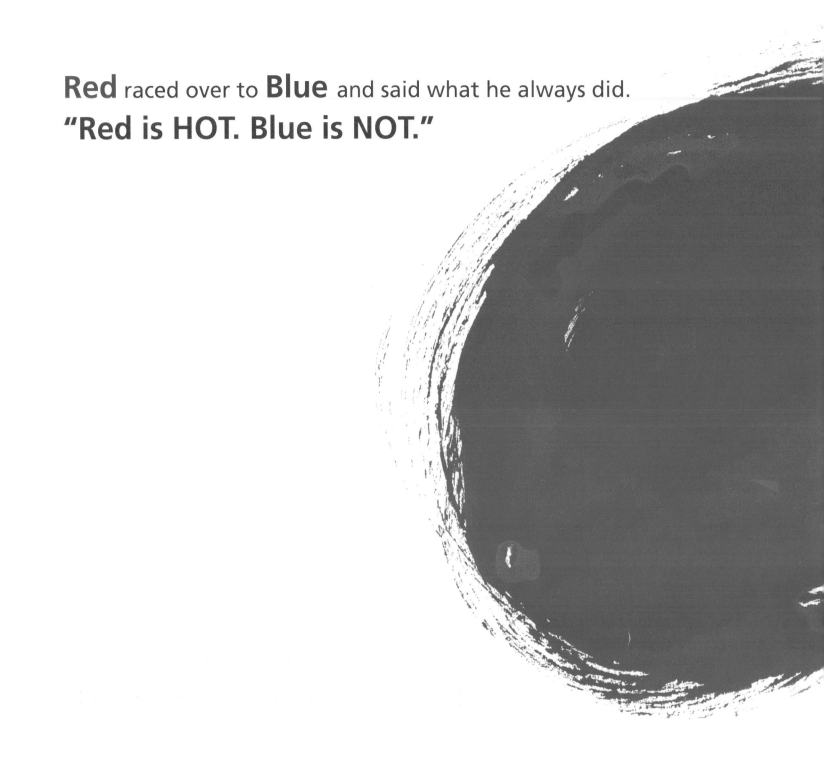

But this time **Blue** stood up tall and became...**SIX**!

"Red can be really **HOT**," he said, "but Blue can be super **COOL**."

Red blew a fuse

and tried to roll over **Blue**!

But everyone took a stand and said,

NO!

1 2 3 4 5 6

Seeing them standing tall, made **Red** feel...

very...

very...

very small.

Then **Red** turned even redder, and began rolling away.

Blue called out,
"Can Red be hot...
AND Blue be cool?"

Red stopped in his tracks.

"Red can count too," said **One**.

Red rocked and rolled and turned into....SEVEN!

"*Everyone* **counts!**" they shouted.

Then **Red** laughed and joined the fun.

Sometimes it just takes One.

To the indy booksellers, my librarian friends and loyal readers. You keep my spirit alive. — K.O.

While it just takes one, it takes more than one to make a book.
Special thanks to Susan McCombs, Amanda Conran, Anne Belden, and Debra Sartell.

Thanks to
those of you who have
shared your powerful stories
of One with me, even
though we have never met.

You make me whole.

- K.O.

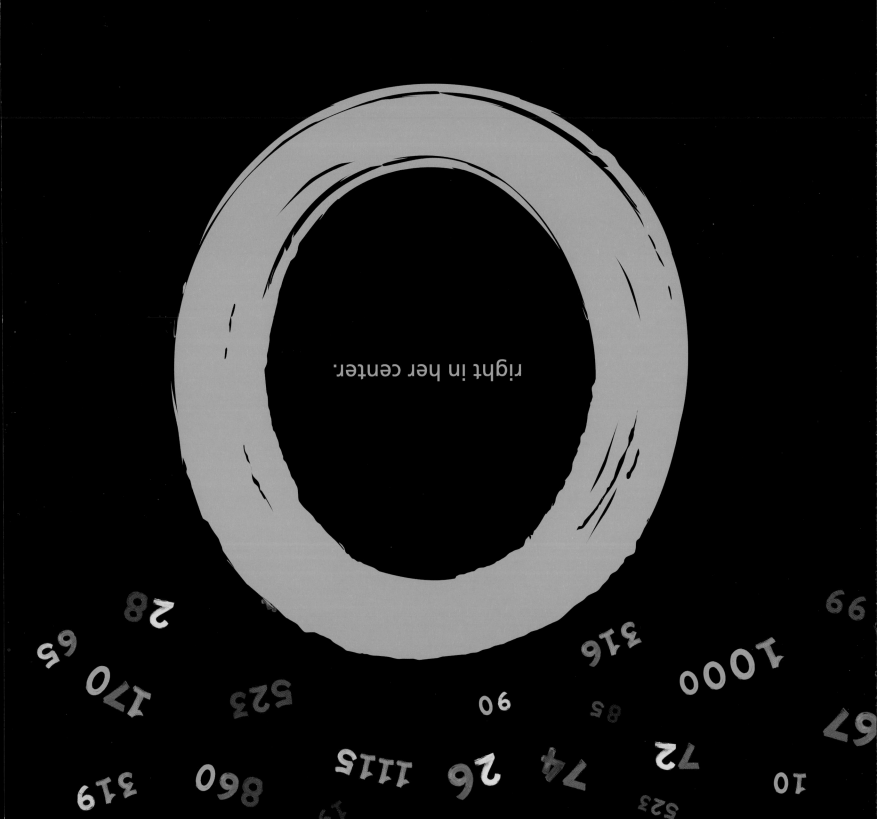

right in her center.

And this time when she looked at herself, she felt whole...

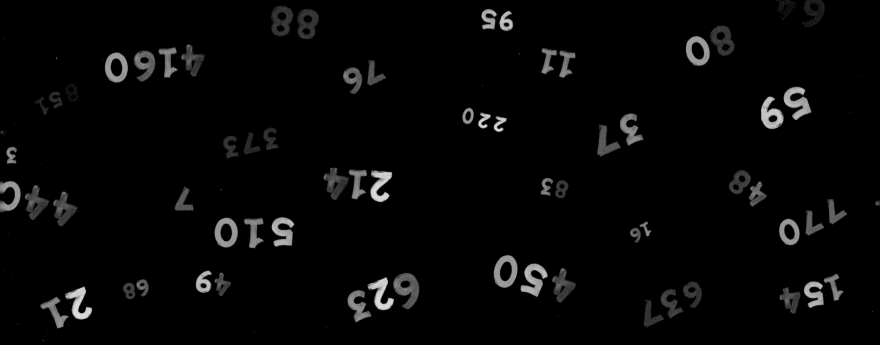

bringing more **value** to everyone.

Zero and the numbers explored and had fun,

"We do count more!" they cheered.

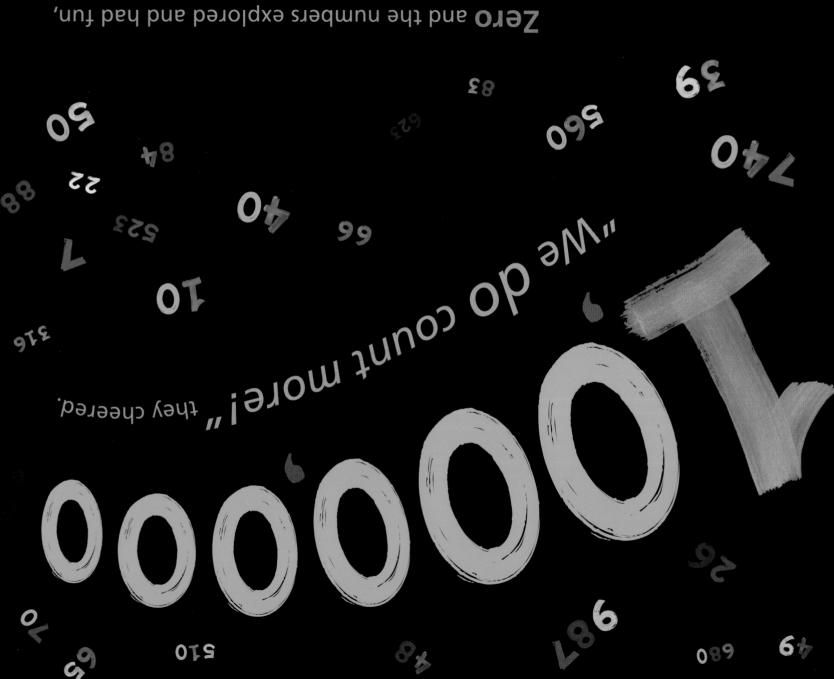

1,000,000

¡1,000,000,001

¡1,000,000,001

¡1,000,001

And what's next?

09

07

08

06

...

If we help each other **soar**, we can count even **more!** Let's **count again** starting with…"

5 6 7 8 9

"Everyone **counts!**" the numbers shouted.

Then she leaped up high and said, "Here's something new we can try!

Zero jumped in.

0 1 2 3 4

Zero rolled up to the numbers.

"I've thought of a way for us to count even *more!*" she said.

"Count more?" asked **Four**.

"Count us in!" exclaimed **Seven**.

"Lead the way!" said **One**.

Suddenly **Zero** saw herself in a new light.

"I'm not empty inside. I'm *open!*"

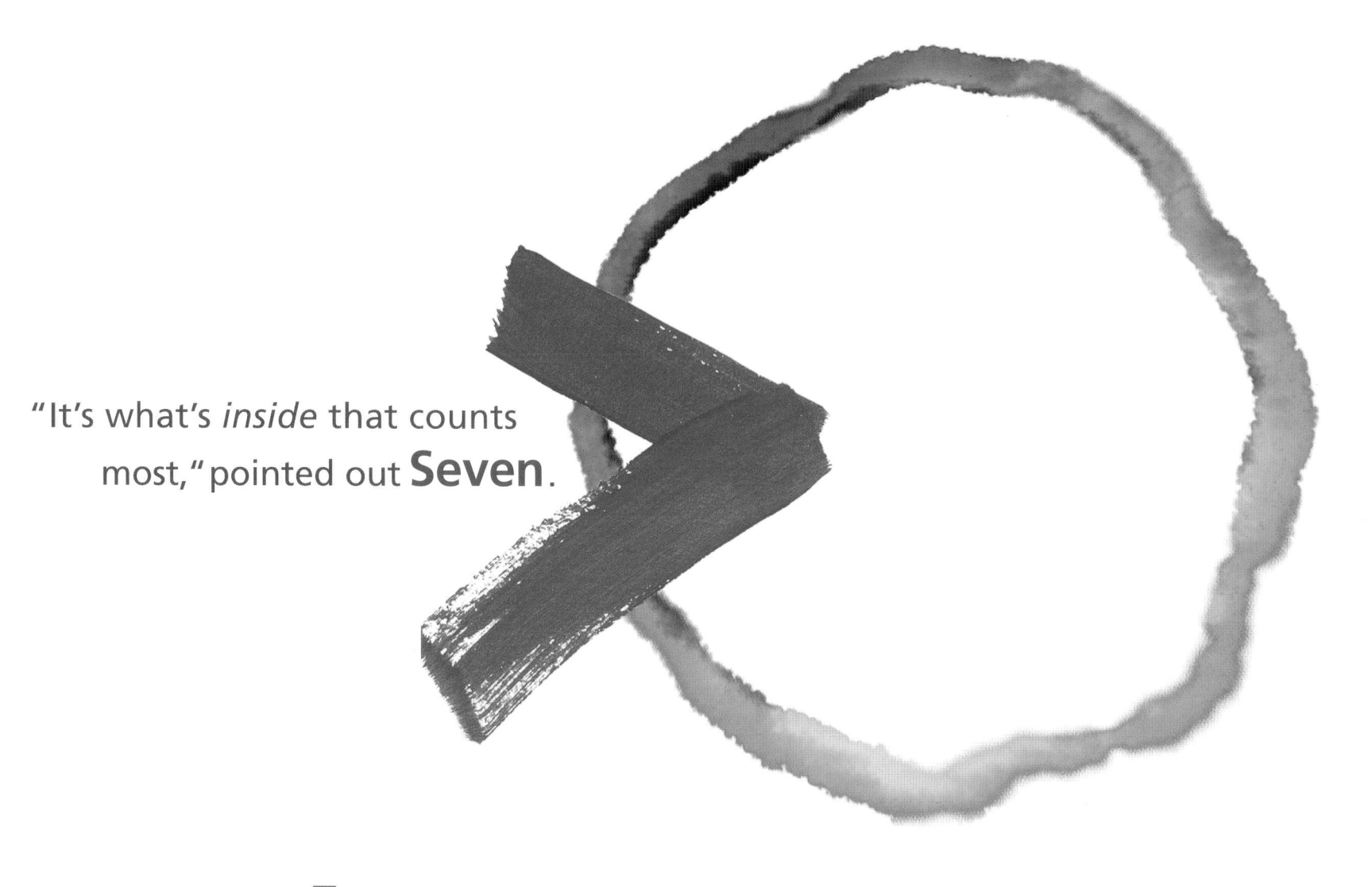

"It's what's *inside* that counts
most," pointed out **Seven**.

Zero looked at herself.
"But…what if I don't have anything inside?"
"Every number has value," said **Seven**.
"Be *open*. You'll find a way."

"It's no use trying," sobbed **Zero**. "I'll never have value. I'll never be part of the count," she said.

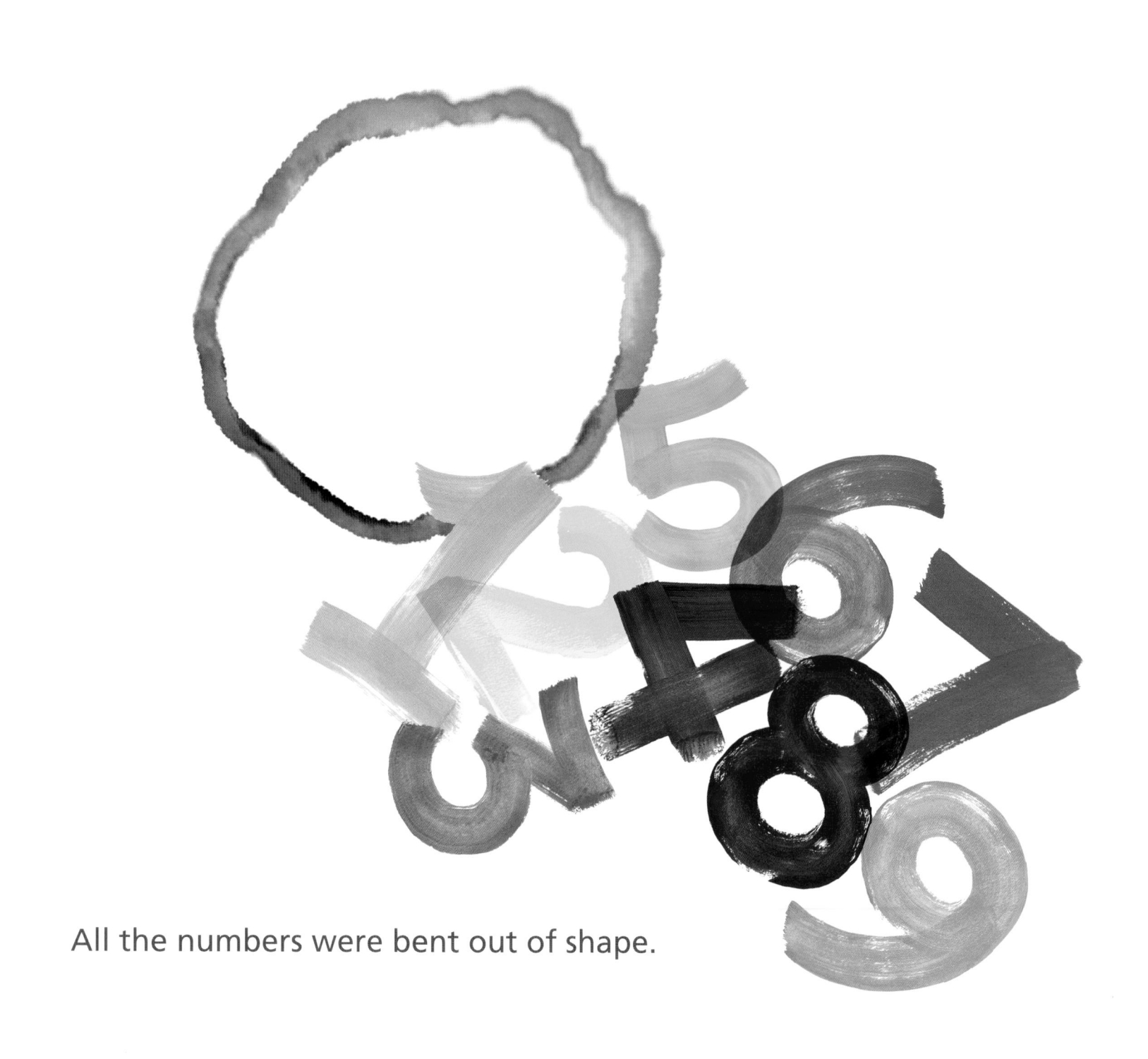

All the numbers were bent out of shape.

right into One,

who knocked over Two,

who fell into Three and Four,

toppling Five and Six,

who crashed into Seven and Eight,

where they all ended up in a big pile on Nine.

and **FASTER!**

She leaped – flying, soaring, rocketing…

Zero had a new thought.

If she could *impress* the numbers, that'd give her **value**.

She'd leap, she'd soar, she'd sizzle, she'd shine.

She'd make a grand entrance and floor them all!

and **faster...**

Zero began to roll **faster...**

"We're on our way to join the others.
Come count with us!" they said.

Zero felt deflated.
Eight and **Nine** were numbers with **value**.
Of course they'd **count**. How could they know how she felt?

But **Zero** could only be **Zero**.

Eight and Nine rolled into the scene.
"If you doubled yourself up, you'd be like me!" said Eight.
So Zero twisted and turned to try to be Eight.

"Or you could be a Nine with a longer line," said Nine.
So Zero pinched and puckered to try to be Nine.

Z

e

r

o

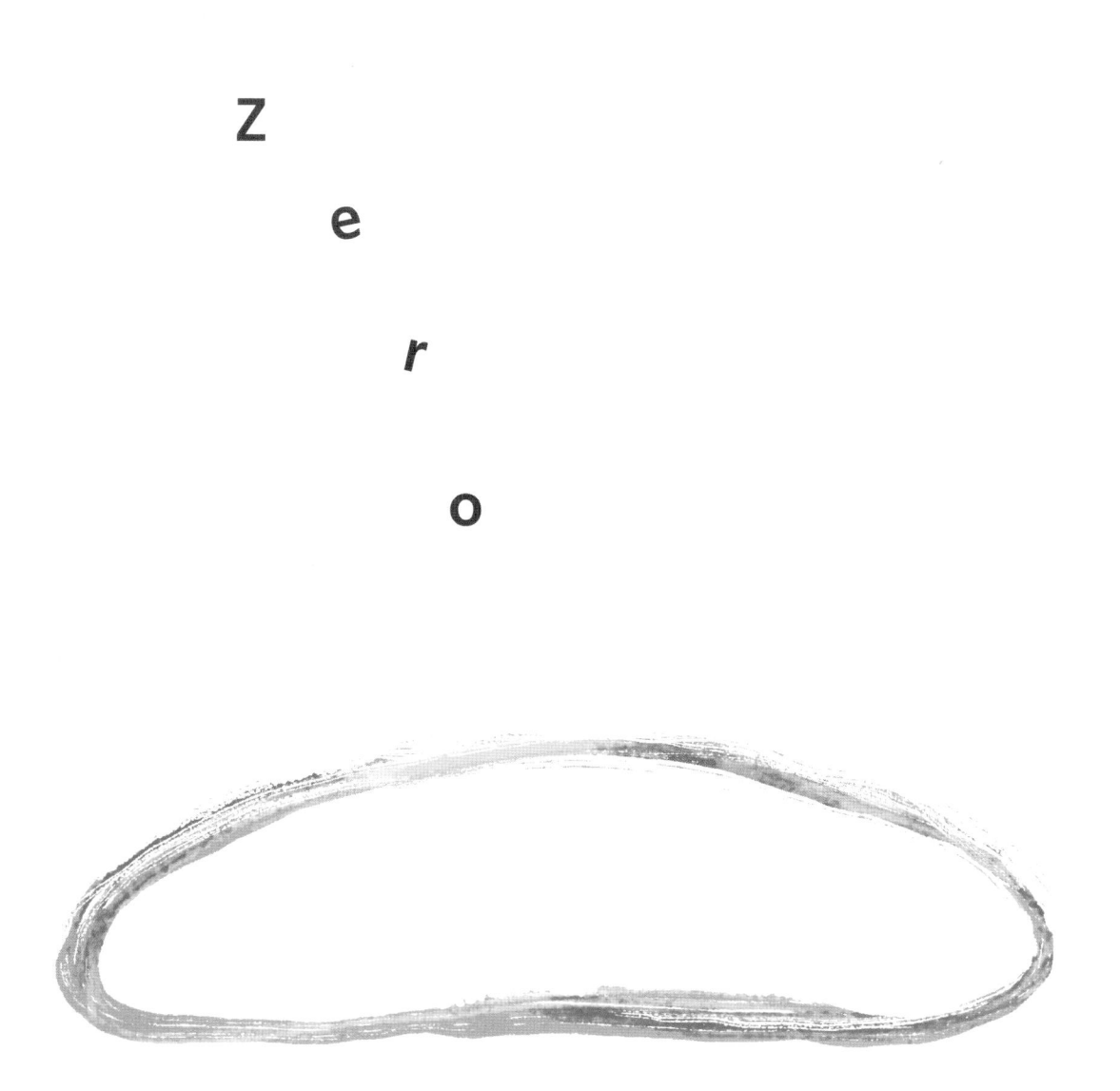

She sighed. Becoming like **One** was too much of a stretch.

she FORCED and FLATTENED and finally became…

So she *pushed* and pulled,

she stretched and STRAIGHTENED,

Zero was big and round with no corners at all.

"If I were like One, then I could count too!" she thought.

One was solid and strong with bold strokes and squared corners.

She watched **One** having fun with the others.

But how could a number worth nothing become something?

Zero felt empty inside.

Every day she watched the numbers line up.

She wanted to **count** too.

When she looked at herself,

she just saw a hole...right in her center.

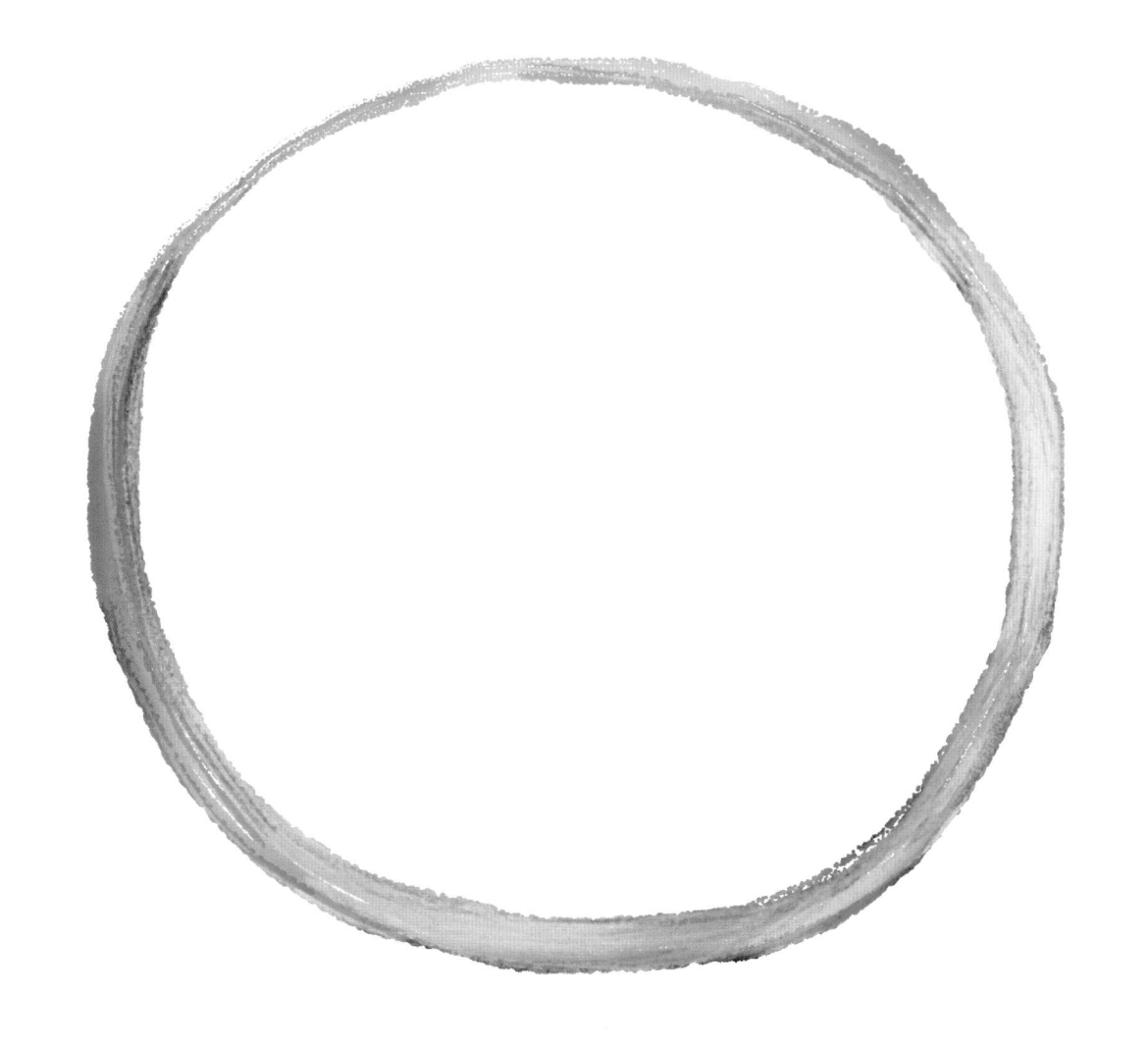

Zero was a big round number.

by Kathryn Otoshi

Zero